CANADA

Minnesota

Wisconsin

Michigan

Iowa

Illinois

Indiana

Ohio

Missouri

West
Virginia

Kentucky

Virginia

Tennessee

Arkansas

Mississippi

Alabama

Georgia

North
Carolina

South
Carolina

Louisiana

Florida

Pennsylvania

New York

Maine

New
Hampshire

Vermont

Rhode Island

Connecticut

Massachusetts

New Jersey

Delaware

Maryland

Washington,
D.C.

New York City

The Twelve Days of Christmas in New York City

written and
illustrated by

Lisa Adams

STERLING

New York / London

Dear Cousin Emily,

It's Christmastime in the city! Mom, Dad, and I are so happy you will be visiting. There are so many sights to see and so much to do! Just for starters—get ready for hot slices of pizza and cold jolly Santas on every corner. We have plans to show you our island of Manhattan and all the other boroughs, too—Brooklyn, Queens, the Bronx, and Staten Island. There's nothing like a twelve-day visit to celebrate the twelve days of Christmas!

When we drive into Manhattan from the airport you'll get an eyeful—all the tall buildings here, there, and everywhere. And I have a surprise for you: I'm going to introduce you to my friend, who happens to be the best tour guide ever. He can fly all over New York! We are going to have an awesome time.

See you soon,
Daniel

Dear Mom and Dad,

Arrived! Daniel and Aunt Gail met me at the airport, holding a huge EMILY sign. Sure helped—there were so many people going every which way. As we drove into Manhattan, I could see tons of skyscrapers. They are even bigger than they look in the movies! We dropped off my bag at Daniel's apartment and walked over to Central Park. Aunt Gail calls it "New York's backyard" because even though most people here don't have their own yards, they can all share this one. I felt like I was suddenly in the country because of all the meadows, hills, lakes, and nature trails. We even saw a gigantic sculpture of the tea party from Alice in Wonderland! Daniel bought me a bag of roasted chestnuts—a favorite street treat here. Delicious! Holding up a chestnut, Daniel called out, "Hey, Mugsy. Here's a snack! Come down and meet Emily." I think that pigeon liked me right off the bat; he swooped to the ground and flapped his wings at me. He's going to be our official tour guide. How cool is that?! I love NYC already.

Love,
Emily

On the first day of Christmas,
my cousin gave to me . . .

a pigeon in a Central Park tree.

Dear Mom and Dad,

Guess who greets you when you walk into the American Museum of Natural History? Mrs. Barosaurus (as tall as a 5-story building), rearing up to protect her baby from a scary meat-eater! Scientists put together their skeletons piece by piece, using casts made from the original fossils. The museum has <u>hundreds</u> of other dinosaurs on display, along with exhibits on just about every animal you can imagine. Daniel's favorite is a HUMONGOUS blue whale—it's 94 feet long!

In another part of the museum, the Rose Center for Earth and Space at the Hayden Planetarium, we saw an incredible show about cosmic collisions—the floor even shook as we watched a "meteorite" zoom to Earth! The real meteorite crash-landed on Earth 65 million years ago and probably caused the Age of Dinosaurs to end. Wow.

To calm down a little, we visited the quiet Hall of Minerals and Gems, back in the main part of the museum. Gazing at the world's largest star sapphire made me forget stomping dinosaurs and blazing meteorites for a while. The gem shimmered like a blue candle and I could really see the star in it.

Emily

On the second day of Christmas,
my cousin gave to me . . .

2 dinosaurs

and a pigeon in a Central Park tree.

Dear Mom and Dad,

Snowflakes fell like whispers all night long, and this busy city is so quiet today. Daniel says that's the perfect time to visit St. Patrick's Cathedral.

With its pointy spires, it looks just like the big churches in Europe I remember from Grandma's postcards. The bells welcomed us as Daniel pushed open one of the huge bronze doors. (He says each one weighs 2,000 pounds. He must be stronger than he looks!) It took my eyes a minute to adjust to the dim light inside the church—everything was so beautiful. There were Christmas decorations at the feet of every statue and even a life-size Nativity scene. Aunt Gail says there are thousands of churches, temples, synagogues, and mosques in NYC—no matter what you believe, you're welcome here.

When we left the cathedral, the snow had stopped, so we rode uptown on a bus to visit Museum Mile. I could have spent DAYS wandering around the Metropolitan Museum of Art. The mummies were the best, but I loved the costumes and the gold and velvet furniture, too. Do you think kids in the olden days got to jump on those super fancy beds?

Love,
Emily

On the third day of Christmas,
my cousin gave to me . . .

3 loud bells

2 dinosaurs,
and a pigeon in a Central Park tree.

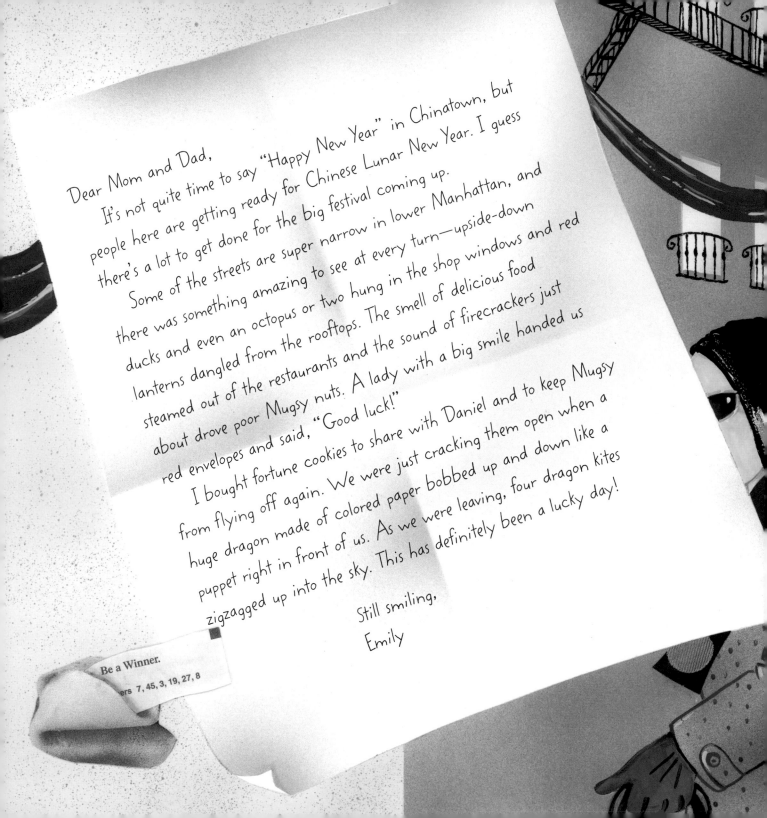

Dear Mom and Dad,

It's not quite time to say "Happy New Year" in Chinatown, but people here are getting ready for Chinese Lunar New Year. I guess there's a lot to get done for the big festival coming up.

Some of the streets are super narrow in lower Manhattan, and there was something amazing to see at every turn—upside-down ducks and even an octopus or two hung in the shop windows and red lanterns dangled from the rooftops. The smell of delicious food steamed out of the restaurants and the sound of firecrackers just about drove poor Mugsy nuts. A lady with a big smile handed us red envelopes and said, "Good luck!"

I bought fortune cookies to share with Daniel and to keep Mugsy from flying off again. We were just cracking them open when a huge dragon made of colored paper bobbed up and down like a puppet right in front of us. As we were leaving, four dragon kites zigzagged up into the sky. This has definitely been a lucky day!

Still smiling,
Emily

Be a Winner.

ers 7, 45, 3, 19, 27, 8

On the fourth day of Christmas, my cousin gave to me . . .

4 dragon kites

3 loud bells, 2 dinosaurs, and a pigeon in a Central Park tree.

Dearest Mother and Father,

Have you ever been INSIDE a fairy tale? I think I was tonight, when Daniel and Aunt Gail took me to see Rockefeller Center. The giant Christmas tree there was decorated with thousands of twinkling lights and had a crystal star on top that seemed as big as the comet we saw at the natural history museum. (A tour guide told us that the star is 10 feet wide and weighs 550 pounds!) Below the tree floated a statue. I thought it was a golden angel holding a torch, but Daniel says it's actually the Greek god Prometheus, who gave fire to humans as a gift. (Nice guy!) In front of him was an ice rink filled with twirling skaters. Rows of huge toy soldiers standing at attention lined the sides. Everywhere we looked, lights sparkled, stars shone, and happy people took pictures of each other.

To get warm we walked up Fifth Avenue to FAO Schwarz, the oldest toy store in the U.S. Daniel found a teddy bear twice his size, and I got to walk up and down the famous dance-on piano keyboard! We lived happily ever after that evening.

Love,
Princess Emily

On the fifth day of Christmas,
my cousin gave to me . . .

5 shining stars

4 dragon kites, 3 loud bells, 2 dinosaurs,
and a pigeon in a Central Park tree.

Hi, Mom and Dad,

We walked across the Brooklyn Bridge today! Aunt Gail told us that when it was finished in 1883, it was the largest suspension bridge in the world. I believe it.

When we arrived in Brooklyn, on the other side of the bridge, we saw rows and rows of brownstones. These are cool stone houses from the 1830s with big front entrances called stoops, where neighbors can sit and talk—like front porches for everyone to use! We had the best view ever. We could see out into New York Bay, which was filled with long barges, fancy cruise ships, and little red tugboats, and up the East River with its many bridges. Millions of people drive, walk, or bike over them or travel through the tunnels to get to and from work every weekday!

Our next stop was the Brooklyn Museum of Art. It has amazing art from all around the world and it's right next to the Brooklyn Botanic Garden, where we walked through a peaceful Japanese garden that has its own pond and footbridge. Daniel says that in the summer, turtles sun themselves here and fish come right up to the surface of the pond to say hello!

Emily

On the sixth day of Christmas,
my cousin gave to me . . .

6 bridges gleaming

5 shining stars,
4 dragon kites, 3 loud bells, 2 dinosaurs,
and a pigeon in a Central Park tree.

Hey, Mom and Dad,

I thought we had a lot of Christmas spirit back home, but New Yorkers may have us beat! All the streetlights are decorated with ribbons and pine branches, and you can't imagine how beautiful the department store window displays are. Artists, like busy elves, have made amazing scenes just for Christmas. Some scenes are old-fashioned, some are way crazy, and some are super high-tech. It's a big New York tradition to walk from store to store all the way up 5th Avenue, just looking in the windows. I feel as though my nose has been pressed up against glass all day! But the reflection of all the different people passing by even topped some of the displays. I'm sure I heard at least 30 languages being spoken on the street just this morning. And as Daniel promised . . . there were Santas on every corner! With their bells ringing and Christmas music in the air, shoppers rushing by with packages and twinkling lights everywhere, it was like looking at the world through my kaleidoscope.

Candy cane kisses,
Emily

On the seventh day of Christmas, my cousin gave to me . . .

7 sidewalk Santas

6 bridges gleaming,
5 shining stars, **4** dragon kites, **3** loud bells,
2 dinosaurs, and a pigeon in a **Central Park** tree.

Howdy, Mom and Dad,

Kids in NYC are so lucky—they get to hang out with reindeer every time they visit the Bronx Zoo! (I looked hard for Rudolph, but I didn't see any reindeer with red noses.)

Two giant Clydesdale horses pulled us around the zoo in a big wagon—the sea lions barked at us as we rode by, but the horses seemed most interested in the flamingos!

My favorite stop was the Congo Gorilla Forest. Watching the gorillas play under the forest leaves and jump from the treetop lookouts was very cool. We were so close to them—just a pane of glass separated us.

Visiting the indoor habitats was like taking a trip around the world. The Asian jungle exhibit was warm and steamy—perfect for the gibbons and tapirs that live there. And the World of Darkness had bats from South America, sand cats from Africa—even desert scorpions that glowed in the dark! We stayed right until closing time. By then we figured it was suppertime for all the animals . . . and us!

G-r-r-r-r-r-r and Z-z-z-z-z-z,

Emily

On the eighth day of Christmas, my cousin gave to me . . .

8 reindeer roaming

7 sidewalk Santas, **6** bridges gleaming,
5 shining stars, **4** dragon kites, **3** loud bells,
2 dinosaurs, and a pigeon in a Central Park tree.

Dear Mom and Dad,

The minute the red curtain opened at Lincoln Center, I knew I was in for a treat. I was finally seeing The Nutcracker performed by the New York City Ballet!

The story is about a young German girl, Clara, who gets a nutcracker doll for Christmas and dreams of a nutcracker prince fighting a fierce battle against a mouse king. There's a lot more to the story, but I want to tell you about my favorite scenes: giant toys came to life, the Sugar Plum Fairy danced in the Land of Sweets, and a Christmas tree grew to be taller than a four-story building right before our eyes. Then imagine beautiful ballerinas as dancing snowflakes in a snowstorm that dropped 50 POUNDS of magical, fluttering paper confetti onto the stage! (I learned that from the ballet program.) At the end, Clara woke up under the Christmas tree with her nutcracker doll in her arms. Lots of kids got to dance on stage. Maybe I want to study ballet after all . . .

Dreamily yours,
Emily

On the ninth day of Christmas, my cousin gave to me . . .

9 ladies dancing

8 reindeer roaming, **7** sidewalk Santas, **6** bridges gleaming,
5 shining stars, **4** dragon kites, **3** loud bells, **2** dinosaurs,
and a pigeon in a Central Park tree.

Dear Mom and Dad,

What could be more bouncy and fun than riding on a subway train? Crowds of people rush on and off through the sliding doors, and when you look out the windows everything just whizzes by. Five million passengers ride the subway every day! (I think most of them were on our train.)

Our stop was in Queens, at the home of the famous Steinway & Sons Piano Factory. Did you know that Henry Steinway made his very first piano in the kitchen of his home in Germany? Like many immigrants from far away, he brought all of his skills to NYC when he moved here. He started his company in 1853, and now Steinway & Sons makes more than 5,000 pianos every year for people all over the world! Daniel and I loved the smell of the wood being sanded and bent into shape. I think our dreams will be filled with the sound of pianos being tuned.

Love,
Emily

P.S. After the factory tour, we ate a yummy lunch in Astoria, Queens, famous for its Greek food. Grape leaves and goat cheese— my new favorite snack!

On the tenth day of Christmas, my cousin gave to me . . .

10 tuners tuning

9 dancers dancing, **8** reindeer roaming,
7 sidewalk Santas, **6** bridges gleaming,
5 shining stars, **4** dragon kites, **3** loud bells,
2 dinosaurs, and a pigeon in a Central Park tree.

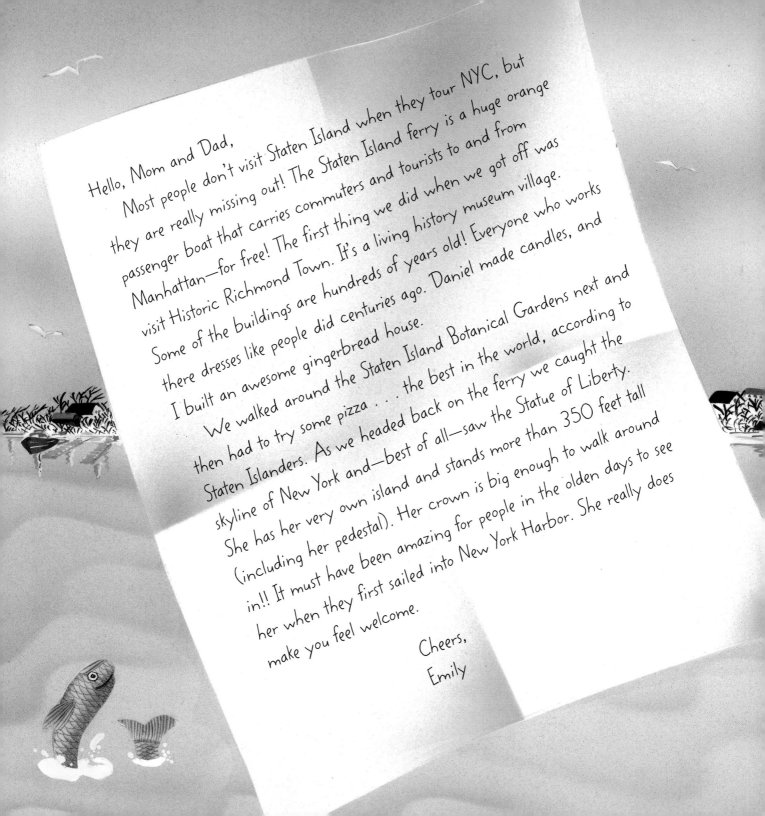

Hello, Mom and Dad,

Most people don't visit Staten Island when they tour NYC, but they are really missing out! The Staten Island ferry is a huge orange passenger boat that carries commuters and tourists to and from Manhattan—for free! The first thing we did when we got off was visit Historic Richmond Town. It's a living history museum village. Some of the buildings are hundreds of years old! Everyone who works there dresses like people did centuries ago. Daniel made candles, and I built an awesome gingerbread house.

We walked around the Staten Island Botanical Gardens next and then had to try some pizza . . . the best in the world, according to Staten Islanders. As we headed back on the ferry we caught the skyline of New York and—best of all—saw the Statue of Liberty. She has her very own island and stands more than 350 feet tall (including her pedestal). Her crown is big enough to walk around in!! It must have been amazing for people in the olden days to see her when they first sailed into New York Harbor. She really does make you feel welcome.

Cheers,
Emily

On the eleventh day of Christmas, my cousin gave to me . . .

11 tourists waving

Staten Island Fer

10 tuners tuning, **9** ladies dancing, **8** reindeer roaming,
7 sidewalk Santas, **6** bridges gleaming, **5** shining stars,
4 dragon kites, **3** loud bells, **2** dinosaurs,
and a pigeon in a Central Park tree.

Dear Mom and Dad,

Tonight will be New Year's Eve! We have plans to celebrate in Times Square with millions of other people, just like New Yorkers have done for more than 100 years. What a great reason to stay up past midnight! We'll have to arrive really early to find a good viewing spot, and Daniel says we'll get all kinds of hats, funny glasses, horns, flags, and paper noisemakers so we can celebrate in style. Every hour there will be a mini-celebration as countries around the world ring in the new year.

Finally, our countdown will begin a minute before midnight, and as we shout out the seconds, confetti, balloons, fireworks, and streamers will fill the air. I really hope I'll be able to see the giant ball drop—it weighs as much as 50 baby elephants. It's all controlled by computer so that the ball, covered with crystals, mirrors, and lights, rotates and drops at exactly the right time. I can't wait!

Happy New Year!
Emily

On the twelfth day of Christmas, my cousin gave to me . . .

12 streamers twirling

11 tourists waving, 10 tuners tuning, 9 ladies dancing,
8 reindeer roaming, 7 sidewalk Santas, 6 bridges gleaming,
5 shining stars, 4 dragon kites, 3 loud bells, 2 dinosaurs,
and a pigeon in a Central Park tree.

New York City: The Big Apple

Some Famous New Yorkers (representing each of the five boroughs):

Alice Austen (1866–1952) was a self-taught 19th-century photographer. Many of her images were taken at "Clear Comfort," her family's Staten Island home. Her photographs offer us a realistic view into upper middle class Victorian life.

Louis "Satchmo" Armstrong (1901–1971) lived in Queens and is buried in Flushing Cemetery. He is widely regarded as the founding father of Dixieland jazz. He played the trumpet and popularized scat singing, using improvised nonsense syllables. He is best remembered for the songs "Hello, Dolly" and "What a Wonderful World."

James Langston Hughes (1902–1967) was an American poet, novelist, playwright, short story writer, and columnist. Hughes is known for his work during the Harlem Renaissance after World War I. Through his writing, he promoted equality, condemned racism, and celebrated African-American culture, humor, and spirituality.

Jennifer Lopez (1969–) was born and raised in the Bronx. She is an accomplished singer, dancer, actress, record and TV producer, designer, and restaurateur. She is best known for her starring role in *Selena* and for her top-selling album, *J. Lo*.

Emily W. Roebling (1843–1903) saved the day in Brooklyn many years ago. The finishing of the Brooklyn Bridge fell into her lap when her husband, the bridge's chief engineer, became ill and her father-in-law, the bridge's designer, suddenly died. Emily learned civil engineering, became a lawyer, and directed and finalized the completion of the bridge.

Eleanor Roosevelt (1884–1962) was born in New York City. Married to Franklin D. Roosevelt, she was First Lady of the U.S. from 1933 until 1945. Mrs. Roosevelt was a relentless advocate for the poor and the working class. She fought to improve women's rights as well as civil rights. Later on in her life, she helped form the United Nations.

Walt Whitman (1819–1892) was an American poet and humanist who lived and worked in Brooklyn, Queens, Long Island, and Manhattan. He is best known for his poetry collection *Leaves of Grass*. Famously kindhearted, Walt Whitman volunteered as a nurse in hospitals for war veterans during the Civil War.

To Gino Hollander, cool beatnik painter;
and John D. Adams, my ad man dad who showed me New York City the right way . . .
zooming around Greenwich Village in the back of an MG.
—L.A.

STERLING and the distinctive Sterling logo are registered trademarks
of Sterling Publishing Co., Inc.

Library of Congress Cataloging-in-Publication Data
Adams, Lisa, 1951-
The twelve days of Christmas in New York City / written and illustrated by Lisa Adams.
p. cm.
Summary: Emily writes a letter home each of the twelve days she spends exploring the five boroughs of
New York City at Christmastime, as her cousin Daniel shows her everything from a pigeon
in a Central Park tree to twelve streamers twirling on New Year's Eve. Includes facts about New York City.
ISBN 978-1-4027-6440-0
1. New York (N.Y.)--Juvenile fiction. [1. New York (N.Y.)--Fiction. 2. Christmas--Fiction. 3. Cousins--Fiction. 4. Letters--Fiction.] I. Title.
PZ7.A21749Twe 2009
[E]--dc22   2008050090

2 4 6 8 10 9 7 5 3 1
06/09

Published by Sterling Publishing Co., Inc.
387 Park Avenue South, New York, NY 10016
Text and illustrations © 2009 by Lisa Adams
The original illustrations in this book were prepared using gouache, colored pencils, airbrush, and collage.
Designed by Kate Moll and Patrice Sheridan
Distributed in Canada by Sterling Publishing
c/o Canadian Manda Group, 165 Dufferin Street
Toronto, Ontario, Canada M6K 3H6
Distributed in the United Kingdom by GMC Distribution Services
Castle Place, 166 High Street, Lewes, East Sussex, England BN7 1XU
Distributed in Australia by Capricorn Link (Australia) Pty. Ltd.
P.O. Box 704, Windsor, NSW 2756, Australia

Printed in China
All rights reserved

Sterling ISBN 978-1-4027-6440-0

For information about custom editions, special sales, premium and
corporate purchases, please contact Sterling Special Sales
Department at 800-805-5489 or specialsales@sterlingpublishing.com.

Brooklyn Botanic Garden® is a registered trademark of Brooklyn Botanic Garden Corporation. All rights reserved.
Coney Island Cyclone® is a registered trademark of Cyclone Coasters, Inc. All rights reserved.
Macy's® is a registered trademark of Macy's Department Stores, Inc. All rights reserved.
Radio City Music Hall Christmas Spectacular® starring the Rockettes® is a registered trademark of Radio City Trademarks. All rights reserved.

Special thanks to Heidi Dettinger, Director of Marketing and Communications at Steinway & Sons.

Washington

Oregon

Montana

No.
Da.

Idaho

Wyoming

Sou.
Dak.

Nevada

Nebr.

Utah

Colorado

California

Ka.

Arizona

New Mexico

Ol.

Hawaii

Alaska

Texas

MEXICO